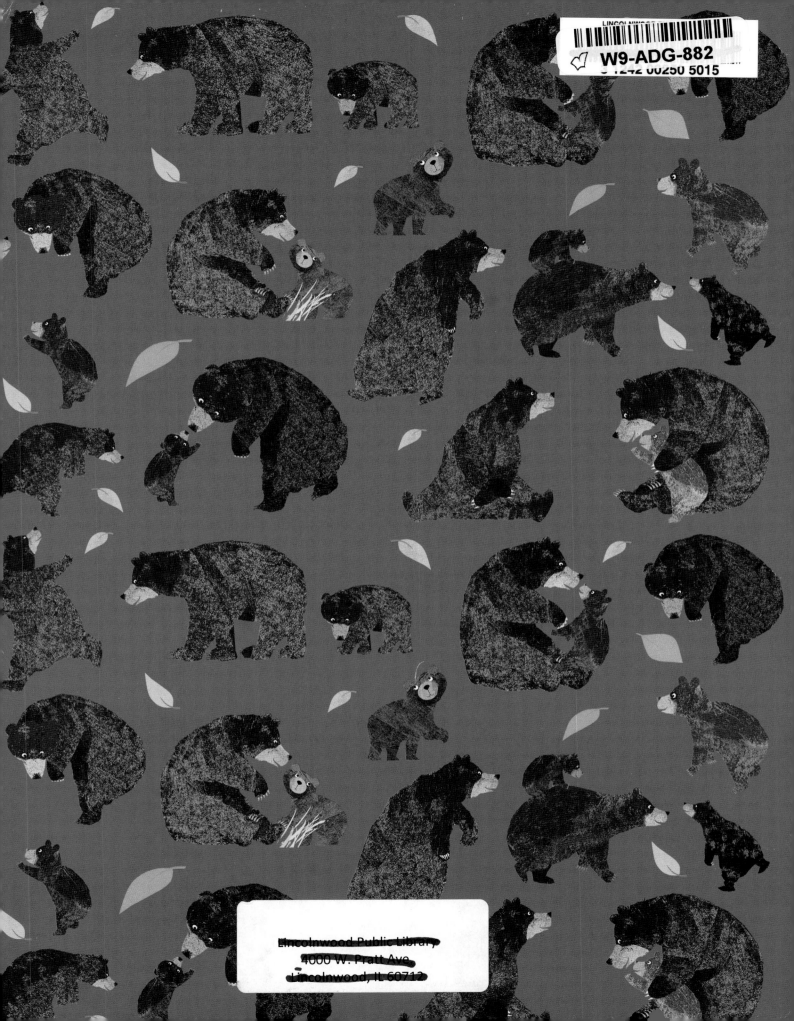

First published in the United States, Great Britain, Canada, Australia, and New Zealand in 2014
by NorthSouth Books Inc., an imprint of NordSüd Verlag AG, CH-8005 Zürich, Switzerland.

Distributed in the United States by NorthSouth Books Inc., New York 10016.
Library of Congress Cataloging-in-Publication Data is available.

ISBN: 978-0-7358-4180-2
Printed in Germany by Grafisches Centrum Cuno GmbH & Co. KG, Calbe, April 2014.
1 3 5 7 9 • 10 8 6 4 2

www.northsouth.com

FSC
www.fsc.org
MIX
Paper from
responsible sources
FSC® C043106

Sleep Tight, Little Bear

Britta Teckentrup

North
South

It was late autumn. The days had grown short, and most of the leaves had fallen from the trees. Soon the whole forest would be covered with snow. Winter was on its way.

Today was to be a great day. Little Bear and Mommy Bear had worked hard, getting their cave ready for their winter sleep.

Little Bear was romping around in the brightly colored autumn leaves. He was very excited. "Mommy, is it true that it'll soon be dark and cold and stormy?" he asked.

"Yes, Little Bear. It will be very dark and very cold and very stormy."

"And when we wake up in the spring?"

"Then it'll be warm again, and the sun will be shining. Come along, we must say good night to our friends."

First, they went to Badger's burrow.

"Hello, Badger," said Little Bear excitedly. "Tonight we begin our winter sleep!"

"Oh yes, it's starting to get cold," answered Badger. "I'll be going to bed soon myself. Sleep tight, and sweet dreams!"

"Sleep tight, Badger!" cried Little Bear.

Then they met Mommy Fox and her cubs.
"Sleep tight, my friend," said Mommy Fox.
"We'll meet again in the spring."
Each of the fox cubs gave Little Bear a
good-night kiss.

They met more friends.
"Good night, Deer!"
"Sweet dreams, darling!"
Deer replied.

"I must hop into my
burrow," cried Rabbit.
"Sleep tight, Little Bear."

"Good night, good night, don't let the bedbugs bite!" giggled the mice, running into their holes.

"Good night, Squirrel!"
"Here's a nut for you from my winter store, as a bedtime treat!"

"Good night, Owl," cried Little Bear,
although he knew that Owl was grumpy.

"Tut! Hoo!" said Owl. "You sleepyheads . . .
lying on your bearskin, while we owls have to
stay awake all night keeping the forest in order."

Then she turned her head all the way around
behind her.

Now old, gray wolf also came and stood before them. "Good night, my dear Little Bear," said Wolf in his deep voice. "I'll make sure that you are safe and well while you are sleeping."

Finally, Little Bear and Mommy Bear sat at the top of the hill and snuggled up nice and close to watch the sun go down. Soon the shadows grew longer, darkness fell, and the smell of snow was in the air. The wind blew so cold that Little Bear shivered. Then Mommy Bear knew the time had come.

"Time for bed, Little Bear," she said.

Inside the cave it was warm and cozy. Little Bear yawned and curled up on the soft leaves. "Mommy, will you stay with me?"
"Forever," said Mommy Bear.

"Mommy," whispered Little Bear, "will you give me one more hug?" Mommy Bear gave Little Bear the sort of hug only a mommy bear can give.

"Mommy, will you give me one more kiss?"
Mommy Bear bent down and gave Little Bear
a very gentle kiss.

"Mommy, . . . " But Little Bear couldn't finish
his sentence, because he'd already fallen asleep.
Mommy Bear couldn't help smiling.

"I love you," she whispered in Little Bear's ear. She curled up right beside him. "Sleep tight, Little Bear." She could hear him breathing softly in and out. And then she fell asleep herself.

Both of them dreamed of the warm sun that would be waiting for them in the spring.

Winter Sleep

Bears sleep most of the time from autumn to spring, waking up now and then to hunt for food. The long rest enables them to save their energy, which is important during the cold season when they can't find much to eat. Cubs stay with their mother for up to two years. Male bears sleep alone.

Squirrels sleep in their nests up in the trees, but they often come down to the ground, looking for food or digging up their winter stores. Badgers rest in their burrows. Their winter sleep can last for a few days or a few months, depending on how cold the weather is.

Most mice don't sleep through the winter. They build up a store of food and find themselves a nice warm place to stay.

Like most birds, owls remain wide awake all through the winter. Wolves, fox, deer, and rabbits grow thick fur to survive in cold temperatures.

What do *you* do in the winter? How do *you* stay warm when it's cold outside?

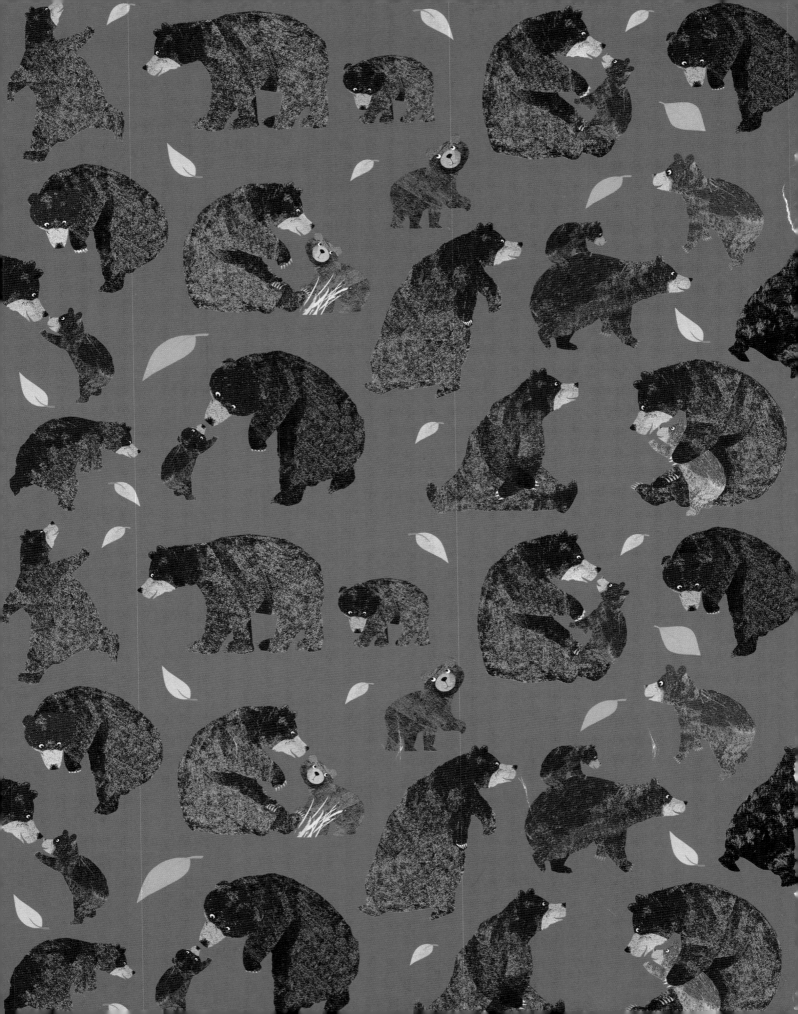